To Mom,
Thanks for everything.
x
Joshua, August 2020

AS ABOVE, SO BENEATH

JOSHUA D. TAYLOR

Available from Black Hare Press in 2020

SHORT READS

WARDENCLYFFE by GREGG CUNNINGHAM
HADES 11 by PAUL WARMERDAM
BLOOD AND SILK by ZOEY XOLTON
AS ABOVE, SO BENEATH by JOSHUA D. TAYLOR
DEAD MAN WALKING by DAVID GREEN
THE RISE OF THE GREAT OLD ONE by JASMINE JARVIS
CHRYSALIS by KIMBERLY REI
MOUNT TERROR by E.L. GILES

UNDERGROUND

MIRACLE GROWTH by TIM MENDEES
THE RETURN by GABRIELLA BALCOM
UNDERGROUND by S. GEPP
WHISPERS IN THE DARK by K.B. ELIJAH
SWIRLING DARKNESS by SAM M. PHILLIPS
THE GATE TO THE UNDERWORLD by E.L. GILES
COLD AS HELL by NEEN COHEN

Twitter: @BlackHarePress
Facebook: BlackHarePress
Website: www.BlackHarePress.com

Edited by D. Kershaw
Formatting by Ben Thomas
Cover design by Dawn Burdett

I found myself standing along a shoreline, cool waves gently lapping against my ankles. The sky was dark as I stared out over the sea. The star's reflection twinkled on its smooth surface. So perfect was the reflection that I could not tell where the night

sky ended and the sea began. I was surrounded by infinite blackness, vast and uncaring. The stars that kept me company were so distant that I could fall through the void for all eternity and never touch one.

Just when the loneliness and isolation began to become too much, at the exact moment, I felt myself about to run screaming into the waves and swimming until my arms and legs grew tired and leaden, and I blissfully sank below the surface. One of the stars moved.

I surged with excitement to no longer be alone. The star moved more quickly and grew brighter and brighter as it approached, burning in the sky until night became day. I shielded my eyes, fearing that my saviour had become my destruction, as it fell from the sky. The bright yellow tail of the comet illuminated the horizon as it crashed into the sea, and for an instant, I saw a queer triangular shape off in the distance. Then all was dark again.

I felt the tide rising around my legs, then looked down. In the pale starlight I found not waves but snails creeping from the water, leaving trails of reeking ichor as they climbed my legs by the dozen. Terror consumed me as they made their way up my body. I tried to run but my feet were stuck in the sand. I tried to scream but could not be heard over the crashing surf.

Nemo Carter awoke screaming in his bed aboard the research vessel the *Silver Key*. He swatted and scratched at his legs, trying to prevent the phantom snails from reaching his body until he realised it had all been a dream. The bed protested as he collapsed back into it, panting. After a moment, he swung his legs over the side and inspected them. They were completely unmolested, though he was sure he could still feel the snails as he ran his hands over them. He cradled his head in his hands as he felt the gentle roll of the sea.

"Why snails?" he asked himself. He grabbed a squeeze bottle of water beside the bed and drank deeply, trying to clear his head. He stood up and walked through the kitchenette next to the bedroom, waving his hand at the coffeemaker to start brewing a fresh pot. He headed up the stairs to the research station that led into the *Silver Key*'s bridge.

Nemo placed his water bottle down on the round display table as the smell of coffee began to waft up from below deck. He had to make a conscious effort not to rub his legs. The dream was so confusing, not just all surreal imagery like the time he had been bitten by a hallelujah fly and hallucinated for three days. The strangest part was that Tindalos did not even have snails or any kind of gastropods at all. They had been completely left out when the planet's terraforming had been planned, in favour of more advanced forms of polychaete worms. He had only ever seen snails when he was in college studying marine biology, where they had been kept under lock and key along with all the other non-native species.

He waved a hand over the display table summoning a holographic image from the 3D sonar scan of the migrating bake-kujira pod. He leaned over, resting his elbows on the table, studying the great slow-moving jellyfish relatives. They were all still there from yesterday, eighteen adults and seven sub-adults, following the flow of plankton down the coastline. The boat had been set to follow them while he slept. They were exactly where he expected them to be on their annual migration route, which was good but did not help him at all. He took another sip of water. He was beginning to feel more grounded now that he was focusing on his research.

The bake-kujira had periodically begun leaving their migration routes to beach themselves on shores.

No one knew why. So, he had been charged by the Tindalos Terraforming Council to find out what was happening to the gentle giants. There was quiet fear that no one dared to voice officially that this could be a sign of terraforming reversal. It happened sometimes. Most of the time when a terraformed world failed, it was in the beginning, the first few hundred years. The world fails to thrive before the terraforming really takes hold. In some rare instances, the terraforming initially seems successful and continues to develop for thousands of years, but there is a flaw. Something that has been there since the beginning completely unnoticed, which causes a cascade effect. Making a perfectly stable planetary ecosystem collapse in on itself, rendering the planet lifeless.

This is what Nemo had been sent to look for. He needed to determine what was affecting the bake-kujira. Then determine if it was part of a larger systemic problem. It was his job to assuage the council's fear of global collapse. Tindalos was only 5,000 years into its terraforming, still in its fragile infancy. Humans had only been colonising it for about 500 years, so it was still possible for a backslide.

On top of everything else, the bake-kujira were a keystone species. The entire ocean's ecosystem depended on their presence. Entire food chains would collapse without them. If something happened to them, it would have an enormous effect on the ocean's ecosystems.

As Nemo stood there, with the scent of coffee calling to him while he stared at the holographic display, he had no idea what was happening. Since he had begun following them almost a month ago, they acted perfectly normal for the giant filter-feeding tubes that propelled themselves through the oceans with a series of hardened combs. This was good news for animals, but bad news for trying to get to the bottom of the mystery. He would just have to keep following them and wait for aberrant behaviour to manifest itself.

He turned to go back below the bow to complete his morning ritual with a cup of black coffee when he saw something out of the corner of his eye. He whirled back to the display, knocking the squeeze bottle to the floor. He had seen a large pyramid at the edge of the hologram. At least he thought he had. Now there was nothing there except for the pod of bake-kujira. He rubbed his eyes again. His dreams were still intruding on the waking world. A sure sign that he needed his coffee.

After he retrieved his spill-proof mug, he heated a bacon-egg-toast ring, and he went onto the bow of the ship where he leaned against the railing. He wished he had remembered bringing sunglasses as he squinted against the bright morning light of the twin suns. He wrapped his arms around himself as he sipped his hot coffee to ward off the cool ocean breeze. He stared into the distance at the spot where the bake-kujira would be placidly filter feeding.

The ship leaned to the right, making a subtle adjustment to keep the pod in front of it. Nemo glanced in that direction and saw several bristled false seals lying on top of the right outrigger, getting a free ride, just like they did with the bake-kujira. They were predatory polychaetes with sinuous metre-long bodies. He would have to scrub the adhesive from their paddles off when he got back home, whenever that would be.

After the suns rose and the air warmed, Nemo went back inside the research station to monitor their course. The holographic satellite image displayed their progress through the warm shallow coastal waters of Hy-Brasil that they had been travelling south along for several weeks. There were no human settlements on Hy-Brasil, just a scattering of research stations farther inland. Most human settlements were in the northern archipelago of Ulthar.

In a couple of days, they would cross the opening to the Sea of Hali to the west, which separates Hy-Brasil from Arcadia, then continue south to the annual breeding grounds. The Sea of Hali was not a feature original to Tindalos but a crater formed by a comet that had been pushed into the planet by early terraformers to provide water and atmosphere thousands of years ago.

Nemo paused, still crunching on his breakfast ring; the comet made him think again of his dream. The great yellow light streaking through the sky had been the source of both terror and adulation. At least now he knew what part of his mind the dream imagery had come from—now if he could only figure out the pyramid and the snails. He decided that he had been spending too much time alone out on the open ocean. He promised himself to call Madeline later that day.

JOSHUA D. TAYLOR

Nemo showered, checked the weather, saw a storm forming too far off at sea to be a concern to him, then returned to the tracking room to go over the data. He compared the migration of other pods with this one. Many of the bake-kujira had trackers on them while others were followed by submersible drones. He overlaid this information with all the locations on the map where the animals were found beached. They seemed to have passed by the Sea of Hali sometime before beaching themselves. Though sometimes it was days, weeks, or even months later. Their migration did not normally take them into the sea itself though. He poked the hologram with his finger. It shimmered in response.

Something about it unsettled him. As far as he could tell, there was nothing there that could be causing the animals' destructive behaviour; but like the phantom snails on his legs, he could not help but feel like something was there, even though logic told him otherwise. Maybe it was not the sea but the comet, he wondered.

A sharp pinging drew his thoughts from his ponderings. A message was coming in; it was Madeline. He accepted the message. The map was replaced with an image of her round face with a warm smile.

"Maddie, I was just thinking of calling you. How are Debbie and the girls?" Nemo asked.

"Debbie's good, working all the time and the girls…well you know, clones will be clones. They're intent on proving that they're not exactly like me." She shook her head.

"They'll grow out of it, they always do. How's the frost cactus harvest going?"

"Good, but we've had a heavy fog we can't shake for days. I hope that none of the crops rot. I'm more concerned about your weather though." Madeline was the Global Weather Foundation's representative to the Tindalos Terraforming Council, aside from being one of Nemo's closest friends.

"Me? Everything looks fine here." He could not imagine what she was talking about but knew better than to question his old friend.

"Check again," she said. With a swipe, her image disappeared, and the satellite map returned. The storm had been small and out to sea a short time ago; now it had grown in size and intensity.

"Holy crap, where did that come from?"

"We're not sure; it's acting very strange and defying all of the projections." He could imagine her biting her lip in frustration. "The damn thing seems to have a mind of its own." He knew the source of the concern in her voice. He brought her hologram back up.

"The council's having a fit, aren't they? Claiming that this is a sign of global instability. The beginning of the end." Nemo crossed his arms and leaned against a console behind him.

Madeline smiled and let out a sigh. "I keep telling you, you should go into politics. You've got the council members figured out."

"Not on your life. I can't deal with those fools,

going into a tizzy every time something unexpected happens. That's your job. I'll stick to research."

"Some days it makes me wish that I'd stayed on Hyperborea instead of letting myself get hauled all the way out here to the Hyades Cluster trying to explain to career politicians that weather is unpredictable by its nature and sometimes a freak storm is just a freak storm." Maddie was one of the few people living on Tindalos who was not born there, a descendant of the original colonists. Madeline was born and raised on Hyperborea, one of the first terraformed planets. So many things had gone wrong there that entire college courses were focused and dedicated to studying it.

"Yeah, I'd rather weather the actual storm," he said, enjoying the freedom that being a researcher allowed him.

"Well, that's exactly what you're going to be doing. I think you should head towards shore right now before you reach the Sea of Hali and find a protected part of shoreline to anchor and wait out the storm." She looked away, probably studying the weather. "You could anchor safely in Night's Plutonian Shore," she suggested. "I'll send you the coordinates."

Nemo shook his head. "I'll lose the pod if I do that. I've been following them for weeks. Got names for them and everything."

"You can send out submersible drones to follow them while you take shelter, so you can find them when the weather clears."

"It could last for several days. It'll be difficult to catch up," he insisted. He paused to soften his demeanour. Maddie was his friend, not his boss. She was only worried about him. "I'll be fine. The *Silver Key* is rated for heavy storms. I'll message you as soon as it's over to let you know I'm alright."

"You better, it'll be M3's birthday." He

smiled; he'd always like Maddie's third clone daughter the best. She reminded him of himself.

"I promise I won't miss it." They spent a few more minutes on idle chit-chat before signing off. He brought the map back up and overlaid the storm's projected path. It was going to hit them right as they passed by the Sea of Hali. "Well shit," he said to himself. He cleared the screen then to begin his preparations. As he turned his back on the display table, he caught a brief glimpse of a pyramid again, hovering in the air. He spun back to face the table, but the phantom was gone again.

He quickly went over to the console and brought up the display table's history for the last five minutes. He saw the end of his conversation with Madeline along with the weather forecast map. There was a brief blip at the end, right as it switched off. Just a brief instance of incoherent static probably due to a residual charge left in the circuit as it powered down. There was no pyramid.

The storm was moving extremely fast. At this rate, it would be on them in less than six hours. He spent the time preparing the vessel by retracting the outriggers. He launched several drones to follow the pod in case they got separated. There was very little information of their behaviour during extreme weather so it would be interesting to see the drones' recordings. Nemo thought they would probably dive down to avoid the disturbance.

After he finished sealing the ship, he secured anything loose on the inside. It looked like it was going to be a rough night with high waves. With the vessel sealed for heavy weather, all of his communication equipment was retracted so he would have no contact with the outside world until the storm passed. Only limited local sensor abilities would tell him about his surroundings from inside the belly of the ship.

He considered synthesising alcohol to calm his nerves but decided it probably would not go well with the rocking of the boat. So instead he prepared an instant dinner of ham with mac and cheese gel cubes, one of his childhood favourites. When he finished his meal, there was little to do since he was confined to the ship's lower quarters. He tried to review data he already collected but a nervous tension he could not shake prevented him from focusing. He knew he was safe from the storm. The boat could withstand any waves and he was far from any rocks, but something left him unsettled.

He paced the confined interior. He tried to take his mind off things by shopping for birthday presents for M3. Perhaps he would take her on a trip to the orbital research station. He smiled to himself knowing that would make her sisters supremely jealous and irritate Madeline.

He began to feel the rock of the boat more

strongly. The gentle side to side roll had become deeper and more dramatic. He shut down the console; in the brief afterimage of the screen, he thought he saw a triangle. He tried to shake the image from his head. Madeline would laugh at him if he told her he was letting his dreams get to him. She always teased him; she said he was the least scientific scientist she had ever met.

Knowing he was not going to accomplish anything further, he decided to go to sleep. He activated the bed gyros to counteract the increased rolling motion of the increasing waves then turned on the sound dampers to cancel out the pouring rain. Nemo pulled his blankets around him. He hoped for less troubled sleep than the night before. The last thing he needed was to be cooped up inside the ship for two days with no communication while plagued by hallucinations.

I stood on the bow of the Silver Key, the wind and rain lashed the violent seas all around. White-tipped waves like mountains rose above me, black waves on a lightless black sky. The wind, rain, and waves were deafening. I was drowning in the sound as much as the water. Thunder streaked overhead but I was unaware. None of these frightened me, though disaster danced all around my tiny vessel. I knew it was only a portent of greater, unknowable things to come.

Two enormous waves gathered on either side, creating a watery valley in front of me. The rain paused as if I was at the eye of the storm and I felt a deep humming vibration through the bow of the ship—a calling—like the whale songs of the Earth. Then a streak of putrid yellow lightning, larger than any laws of nature would have allowed, lit up the entire world. My eyes burned and retinas contracted in vain. Tears joined the drops of rain running down my face, but I did not look away. I could not. I would not.

Between the mountains of seawater stood the pyramid. Great and terrible, illuminated for a moment by the lightning, but the image burned itself into my corneas. It called out with a subtle, untranslatable song. Then it was dark again and waves crashed down upon me. I was surrounded, crushed, and suffocated. The whole world was darkness—darkness above and below. The only thing that remained was the call, terrible and unavoidable.

Nemo awoke staring up at the ceiling below bow of his ship. It was pitch black and the air was hot and thick. His limbs were heavy. He had trouble sitting up in bed. The air was rank with sweat. His lips cracked when he yawned. This was all wrong. The ventilation and lights were out. He felt about for his water bottle next to the bed and brought it to his lips. It was warm but the wetness soothed his lips and throat.

He took a few deep breaths to steady himself, but instead, he grew lightheaded and faint. The ship was sealed against the storm and the ventilation was down so the below-bow area must have become dangerously low on oxygen. He needed to get the ventilation running and open up the ship. There was no telling how much time he had left. He stopped straining to see in the inky blackness and closed his eyes. He visualised his surroundings since he knew where everything was located.

With his hands outstretched, he made his way to the opposite end of the room to locate the panel for the ship's power grid and transducer. He pulled the handles to pop the panel off. He reached inside to feel if the breaker had been tripped. It would have taken an enormous electrical charge for that to happen—like a bolt of lightning. Nemo reset all the switches, so the lights came on while fresh air swept into the room, removing the stench of his own decay. With relief, he collapsed against the bulkhead, taking great gulping breaths as if he had just been held underwater. He noticed that some, but not all, of the consoles around him were flickering back to life. "What the fuck?" he asked himself.

When he got back to his feet, he drank more water, emptying the bottle. He was so thirsty and hungry. He couldn't understand why. Those were not symptoms of carbon dioxide poisoning. As soon as his immediate needs were met, he sat down to one of the still-functioning consoles to open up the ship so that he no longer felt like he was living in his own tomb. He did not care if the storm was over or not. He liked being out at sea because of the freedom of the wide-open spaces. His near-suffocation below bow on his own exhaled gases was his worst nightmare.

Nemo stopped dead in his tracks, hands hovering over the screen, when he saw the ship's clock. He had assumed that he had been asleep for a single night then awoke sometime the next day. It had been over thirty-six hours since he had gone to sleep. He sat back in his chair, staring at the screen, trying to make sense of things. Perhaps lightning struck near the ship, knocking all of the electrical systems out; without ventilation, the oxygen levels continued to drop, putting him into a coma-like state.

The computers went offline early in the storm, so he had no data at all for almost thirty hours—thirty hours where he'd lain in the belly of the ship like a coffin being tossed about by the sea. The explanation was hardly satisfying, though it explained why he had been starving and dehydrated.

He checked the passive external sensors while he activated the unsealing process and extended the outriggers. The data from the sensors indicated that the weather was warm and sunny. It required several minutes to reconnect with the satellites to establish communications. He frowned. While Nemo was able to receive data from the satellite, such as the weather forecast and communications from the colonies, he was unable to broadcast or send anything out. He rubbed his chin in frustration; he had no way to let anyone know what was happening.

He pulled up a satellite map of the storm. Just as projected, it had collided with him just as the *Silver Key* reached the opening to the Sea of Hali. Then it seemed to stop, losing all forward momentum and just sat there, churning the ocean and battering his ship. Nemo could not imagine what would cause such a thing. It did not make thermodynamic sense. Then after almost twenty hours and sitting still, the storm simply dissolved. Nemo stared in disbelief.

"What the hell is going on?" he asked himself.

He wished he could call Madeline to get her opinion on this seeming impossibility, but with no way to send a message out, he would have to wait until he was able to get the communication systems working again. That did not appear to be anytime soon. He wondered how long he would have to be out of communications with her until she sent someone looking for him. He was hundreds of miles away from any of the usual travel routes since most of Hy-Brasil was uninhabited.

Nemo sat back in his chair. He had no ability to reach anyone. There was no immediate danger now that the freak storm was gone, so returning to his research made the most sense. He walked over to the stairs that led above bow for the first time since the storm passed. There were puddles of water on the steps. Nemo checked the door seals, looking for leaks, but everything seemed to be in perfect working order. He was mystified how water from the storm got inside while the ship was sealed up. He remembered his dream, standing outside on the bow of the ship while the storm raged around him.

He tried to shake the image from his head, but it seemed burned into his frontal lobe. He could almost feel the giant dark pyramid looming over him, dwarfing even the tidal waves on either side. There is no way he would have unsealed the ship to walk outside in the middle of the storm. That would be suicide. He followed the trail of puddles up the stairs, through the research station, and into the bridge where they stopped at the door to the outer bow.

His heart began to pound in his chest as he rested his forehead against the cool metal of the door. Was he losing his mind? He didn't know if he could trust himself.

He distracted himself from unanswerable questions with the more practical matter of cleaning up the water then establishing contact with the drones that were following the bake-kujira. The pod had continued to move south along the coast while he was being tossed by the storm, nearly suffocating. They were a few hundred miles south of his location, right where they ought to be at this part of their journey. If he set the *Silvery Key* at full speed, he should be able to catch up with them before they rounded the continent's southern tip.

However, that was not what Nemo was going to do. As he stared at the floating map, he received yet another shock. Several drones were well into the Sea of Hali following a smaller group of the animals that had broken off the main pod. They must have gotten confused during the storm then headed into the sea in a panic. It made no sense to Nemo. The Sea of Hali had lower salt content that the giant invertebrates preferred due to all the rivers that drained into it from surrounding mountains. They must have been driven into it by something. Or lured in.

This aberrant behaviour was just the thing that Nemo had been waiting to document. Whatever caused them to go off course might be what caused the others to beach themselves. If that was happening, maybe he could prevent it or at least learn from it. Nemo brought up the rogue bake-kujira's coordinates then entered them into the navigation system. This group did not have the ocean current to speed them along, so they moved slower than the main pod. If he travelled at full speed, he would be able to reach them in eight hours. He confirmed the coordinates and activated the ship's engines.

The acceleration caused him to grab the edge of the table for balance. He was just glad the engines were still working. If things got too strange, he could always leave and go home. He was troubled by the thought that he would not know what was too strange until it was too late to turn back. He sighed, then got a whiff of his body odour. He would use some of the eight hours to shower. He hoped that would help set his mind right.

After a thorough scrubbing, Nemo felt more clear-headed and able to tackle the mystery before him. The nagging feeling in his mind that something was off had dissipated. He fortified himself with a meal of fermented kelp then washed it down with hot ginger tea. The tea was so spicy, it made his eyes water: the sort of thing his mother prepared for him when he was sick as a child.

He went back to the display table to see how close he was to the rogue bake-kujira. The *Silver Key* had passed through the mouth of the Sea of Hali, heading as the crow flies towards the five lost individuals. Video feed from the drone revealed two adults and three sub-adults, each larger than his ship. Their behaviour was troubling. They often zigged and zagged, sometimes doubling back only to turn around then continue deeper into the sea, as if they wanted to re-join the others but could not bring themselves to do it.

Nemo wondered what could be causing this strange behaviour. Surely if the freak storm had driven them into the sea, they would have regained their bearings after it passed, but their behaviour continued to be erratic. He chewed his lip.

He wondered if it was some sort of environmental contaminants that affected the bake-kujira. Being massive filter feeders, they were the top of their food chain, so any containment, whether it be biological or chemical, would accumulate in them. Tests had been run on every part of the planet imaginable, the air, water, and soil, since before the terraforming had begun thousands of years ago. Nothing had ever been detected.

He thought about the Sea of Hali and the comet

that created it. The comet had brought water, air, and the very possibility of life to Tindalos. He wondered if something could have been in the comet. Perhaps the comet could have carried some foreign agent to the world with it that was only now making itself known. The idea was madness, but he was beginning to feel like these were mad times.

What would it mean for Tindalos if it turned out there had been a grain of sand in their precisely tuned machine all along? Just waiting to get caught in the right gears to throw the system off and cause the entire apparatus to fall apart. The idea was horrific and tantalising at the same time. Nemo knew he should be using his time to pursue more realistic avenues of investigation until he reached the pod, but he could not help himself.

He searched the ship's database for information on the comet that was used in the planet's terraforming. He was surprised to find out that it had been the largest of eight comets in a ring, given the uncomfortable name, Hastur's Crown. He supposed that Tindalos' comet must have been the crown jewel. Astral phenomenon was not his specialty, but it seemed unlikely to him that comets would naturally form a ring.

As Nemo read the entry, he found that the ring was indeed an artificial structure left by a long-lost alien race, the Leng. The Leng were known for creating truly colossal structures that could be found throughout the known galaxy, which had no discernible purpose. They were assumed to be giant works of alien art, but there was no way to know for sure. The Leng left no other record of their existence. With no idea of who they were or what their goals were, he would never know what the purpose of the comet was. The R'lyeh Corporation had chosen it for the Tindalos Project because of its large size and composition matching what had been requested by the Tindalos Terraforming Council.

Nemo sat there, watching the millennia-old holographs of the comet rotate in front of him. There was something about it that made him feel deeply uneasy—a sense of smallness, helpless in the face of something vast and insurmountable. It was the same feeling he had in his dream, if it had been a dream, looking out at the strange pyramid in the sea.

At the same time, something inside him almost wished to be made to feel helpless, to have his true insignificance in the greater scheme of things shown to him by a greatness so far beyond his existence that it did not even notice him.

None of this made him feel better about the comet and the bake-kujira's strange behaviour. The more he stared at the image, the more he became convinced that it must have something to do with the comet. If he could only divine what its purpose had been. He could almost feel something looking back at him out of the old image. Was there a pyramid inside the ball of ice? He leaned back and rubbed his eyes. He clearly needed coffee and fresh air.

He turned to go back into the bottom of the ship to make another cup of coffee. The tropical parts of the planet had been producing passable coffee for a few hundred years. Nemo was partial to the Kadathian blend from the volcanic highlands. Before he left the tracking station, an idea popped into his head. He tried to cast it aside and focus on the pleasures of a hot cup of coffee being sipped while sea breezes blasted by him as the ship cut through the waves. But he could not. It hung there, burnt into his mind's eye like the afterimage on the console screen. When he searched for "pyramid," he was buffeted with a deluge of information about the pyramids of Old Earth cultures that used the architectural feature. These were well studied and held no mysteries or useful information for him.

They were most commonly used as tombs for the honoured dead and places to worship long-forgotten gods. Many cultures since then had emulated the building style on countless worlds across dozens of solar systems.

Nemo chastised himself for his flight of fantasy but stopped when he saw a pyramid looking back at him: a pyramid with a single eye that glowed on the screen; its eyebrow raised in a question, as if daring him to continue. The all-seeing eye, also known as the eye of providence, floated in front of him. The pyramid with a single eye staring from just below its pinnacle sent chills down his spine. The sense of inescapable observation resonated with everything he had been feeling. This was the pyramid from his dreams. The symbol of an infinite power constantly watching him made him want to hide in his bed and pull the sheets over his head.

He switched off the display then walked

downstairs. Several minutes later, he was standing outside on the bow sipping his dark, bitter coffee. He had to hold onto the railing as the sea breeze and salt spray slipped past him as the ship rapidly closed the distance to the rogue pod. He looked ahead, out over the crystal blue waters of the Sea of Hali. He had to admit that it was quite beautiful. The horizon seemed somehow further away, stretching out to infinity.

Off in the distance, he could see green wisps of sky fruit in front of the white fluffy clouds, not yet so heavy that they rained down into the sea, causing a feeding frenzy of marine life. He sipped his coffee and checked his ETA. It was just over an hour until he caught up with the pod. Then the real work would begin. He would get as close to the pod as they would allow and use every piece of sensor equipment on the *Silver Key* to study them, looking for any sign of what might be causing their behaviour.

A blaring alarm drew his attention—a whining

cry that went from low to high that was impossible to ignore. He hurried to the bridge, placing his spill-proof mug of coffee on a tabletop. The console flashed red in a pattern that indicated an incoming message. Nemo knew it must have been Madeline. He had never contacted her after the storm. If she did not hear from him soon, she would probably send someone to look for him. Even if he returned to base now, it would take him weeks to get there. He needed to see what the bake-kujira were doing right now. What happened next could reveal the answer to their unexplained beaching. There was no turning back for him. He played the message.

"Nemo, are you receiving this? If so, please reply. It's been a couple of days since the storm passed and we still haven't heard from you. Your ship's locator stopped transmitting during the storm, so I don't know where you are. If you're in trouble you need to let me know so I can send help." She bit her lip, trying to keep her emotions from overtaking her. "If I don't hear from you in another two days, I'm going to send M1 and M2 out in the *Rare and Radiant Maiden* to find you. I hope you're okay."

He sat back in his chair and smiled. At least he could depend on Madeline to always act as expected, even if marine animals and the weather seemed to operate on their own set of rules. He would have to apologise to the two young women when they tracked him down in the middle of the sea. It would probably take them weeks to find him. By then he hoped to have some real data on what was happening to the bake-kujira. Madeline would be mad at him for a long time for making her worry, but there was nothing he could do. She would understand in the end. He hoped.

A different alarm blared, more urgent. Nemo left the bridge for the tracking room, forgetting his coffee on the table. This time a console was winking yellow at him. It was an alert from the *Silver Key*'s sensor. They were picking up strong infrasound waves in the sea. He scratched his head. This was surprisingly mundane. With hallucinations and freak hurricanes, he had been expecting something a bit more grandiose. The data that came in indicated that the sounds were similar to sonar—oddly regular for a natural occurrence, but not impossible.

Nemo sat back and reached for his coffee, only to realise that he left it on the bridge. Disappointed, he turned back to the console. Infrasound did occur naturally, sometimes caused by the shifting of tectonic plates. The plates had been punched by a comet when it fell to Tindalos thousands of years ago. The impact could have caused some type of structural damage to the plates. Thousands of years was a blink of an eye in geological time, so it would make sense if they were only seeing the effects of the impact on the planet's subsurface now.

Extremely low-frequency sound waves were known to cause health effects, including paranoia and confusion. The lower the frequency the sound wave, the farther they could travel, even farther through the water. That would explain the bake-kujira's strange beaching behaviour and his own hallucinations.

Nemo was filled with excitement. He made a quick note to cross-reference any other odd animal behaviour, especially sea life, in the vicinity of the Sea of Hali. He was deeply relieved to know that he was not losing his mind. He thought that maybe he would synthesise some alcohol to celebrate.

Nemo tapped at the symbols on the console, using the incoming sensor data to triangulate the infrasound's origin. A thick red band painted itself across the map, leading from his location towards the centre of the sea. He then plotted the bake-kujira's course overtop. Despite veering from side to side and sometimes doubling back, they appeared to be following the red band. His theory confirmed; Nemo felt a deep sense of satisfaction. The mystery that had eluded him for weeks was finally within hand.

He just needed one last detail. He had the ship's computer extrapolate the most likely course the bake-kujira would take based on their present trajectory. Nemo watched a dotted line cut through the centre of the red bar, passing through the spot where the infrasound was originating from. They were headed straight to the source of the infrasound, just like children following the pied piper.

He made another note to suggest a full subsurface geological survey of the Sea of Hali's floor to the Tindalos Terraforming Council when he returned to civilisation.

Nemo began combing through what little data he had available on the effects of infrasound on wildlife and humans. He was cross-referencing the behaviours exhibited as a side effect with any reports of observed behaviours in humans or animals for all of Tindalos' history when an irregular thud interrupted the rhythmic pounding of the waves of the ship's speeding hull. Even out in the deep sea, far from the land, he occasionally bumped into debris. Probably a dead animal or tree trunk. Then there was another impact, and then another. The ship began to automatically reduce its speed as the small collisions continued.

Nemo went to the bridge, slid open the door to the bow, then stepped out into the bright sunlight. He was not greeted by the invigorating smell of briny sea air like he expected. The air was heavy with the odours of putrefaction and rot. His hand went to his mouth, but nothing could protect him from the stench. All around the *Silver Key*, the deliquescing corpses of dead marine animals bobbed about in the gentle waves. The density was so thick that the water was no longer blue but resembled a thick brown soup that would be served only in the very depths of hell.

Nemo's eyes watered as he spun about, desperately seeking an expanse of water devoid of the dull eyes and stiff bodies. He searched for a stretch of the sky not filled with scavenging shantak birds. The air was filled with the sound of hundreds of chitinous wings beating. This made it hard for him to think. They blotted out the sun with their opalescent bodies as they carried off chunks of dripping flesh.

Nemo ran back inside to the bridge, slamming the door behind him. He took great gasps of filtered air. He tried to force out the taint of death from his mouth and nostrils, but he could not get rid of it. It seemed to have gotten behind his eyes to infiltrate his brain. The stench would not let him go. He choked, coughed on it, trying to purge it from his lungs. He retched and finally felt free. He took more deep breaths; the acidic smell of his vomit like a floral bouquet compared to the malodorous air that lay outside.

Nemo collapsed into a chair. The ordeal had lasted only seconds but had completely drained him. It was not simply the visceral shock that shook him to his very core but the utter and instantaneous destruction of the reassuring calm that he had constructed around himself like a cocoon when he thought he had found a rational explanation for everything that was happening. That had been ripped from him like a warm jacket in the middle of a blizzard, leaving him bare and exposed.

After several minutes of staring at the blank consoles in front of him, Nemo's mind slowly gathered around one realisation. He would keep going. There was no other option. He would follow the bake-kujira to reach the end of this mystery no matter how many corpses he had to wade through.

He accepted that the infrasound was calling him just as it was the pod. He supposed he was lucky that he had not ended up like all the other animals, floating, pale and bloated, in the ocean around him. He felt somehow chosen. As if he was destined to uncover what lies there.

He walked back out onto the bow and placed his hands on the railing. He leaned into the breeze. The constant reek of decay buffeted him like a heavy perfume. Nemo knew he would find the pyramid soon. He would stand in its shadow to allow its all-seeing presence to show him what it truly meant to be insignificant.

Time passed quickly for Nemo as he neared his destination. A sense of urgency grew in him. Another message from Madeline arrived. No doubt another insistence that he contact her immediately. He dismissed the message without reading it. It no longer mattered to him. All that mattered was what lies ahead.

Slowly, in the distance, a single point began to rise from the sea as the ship continued to glide across the putrid broth that was the Sea of Hali. The mysterious seed that all this had bloomed from had finally shown itself. Nemo slowed the speed of his approach then returned to the tracking station to check on the pod. On the ship's sonar, the bake-kujira could be seen circling an enormous object with a square base where the infrasound was coming from. A tiny thread of Nemo still knew that it was his job to look after the animals. He wanted them to be okay, even though he knew that nothing would ever be okay again. He held onto the hope that if he could just save them, then at least one thing in the world would be alright.

As the thing he had been seeking came fully into view, Nemo realised that it was not truly a pyramid, but a mountain. A colossal snail shell painted in putrid yellow with a dark circle towards the top, reaching towards the heavens. It towered out of the sea in a way that defied explanation; the spiralling shell blocked out the sun. In the waters surrounding it, the bake-kujira swam in unending circles. They twisted themselves in figure-eights so tight they nearly tied themselves in knots. Eventually, their small minds would become so overwhelmed that they fled the gargantuan snail— swimming with all their might till they died of exhaustion or beached themselves. They were not worthy of its ancient, indifferent gaze.

Nemo stood on the bow. He stared up in terrified awe as the *Silver Key* gently drifted to the cavernous opening in the shell. This close to the titanic mollusc, the infrasound was so intense that his hands vibrated on the railing. The sounds were no geological phenomenon but the reverberations from internal chambers large enough to hold entire towns.

As he docked the ship at the aperture to the shell's interior, he saw many layers, laid down over many millennia of the creature's existence. He climbed down the ladder onto the smooth interior of the shell. He felt a slow, gentle breeze moving in and out. It was the creature's breath. He walked forward, tears streaming from his face; the truth about humanity's insignificance was laid bare before him. There was nothing he could do to even make this monstrosity aware of his existence, let alone stop it from disrupting the natural order of the world he loved so much.

The light from the sun was swallowed up quickly in the place. It only illuminated a few feet inside. Still, Nemo was able to make out aberrations in the otherwise smooth calcareous material of the shell. He drifted over as if in a dream, to see what they were. The scientist that was at the core of him was shell-shocked but still functional. The rough outline of a human skull stared up at him, the outline softened by several layers of shell coating it. All around him were scattered bones of humans as well as others that were completely unfamiliar to him—doubtlessly acquired from some alien world long before humans learned to rub two sticks together to make fire.

He understood that this monstrosity, whose edge he was perched upon, was the true master of Tindalos and always had been. The Leng had sealed it away. Humanity, in their hubris, had freed it, in their desire to make the entire universe suitable for themselves. They had thought themselves the masters of creations and had inadvertently freed one of its true masters.

It had been imprisoned for countless eons inside a comet. Then it survived the impact on Tindalos' barren surface. It went on to live undiscovered in the sea for thousands of years. He knew there was no hope, no free will when an entity like this drifted through the cosmos as arbitrarily as a leaf across the surface of a pond. How could any of their lives have any real meaning in the face of utter undeniable insignificance?

He walked ahead into the darkness, abandoning all hope—to become one with greatness.

65

ABOUT THE AUTHOR

JOSHUA D. TAYLOR *started writing a few years ago when he realised he was too old to play make-believe. He lives in southeastern Pennsylvania with his wife and a one-eared cat. He enjoys gardening, comic books, ska-punk music, Disney World, and traveling with his wife.*

Raised during weirdness that was the late 20th century, Josh's eclectic interests produce eclectic works. He loves to mix-n-match things from different genres and story elements to achieve a madcap hodgepodge of the truly unexpected.

Bibliography

APOCALYPSE, Black Hare Press 2019
Athena, Dastaan World Publishing, 2020
BEYOND, Black Hare Press, 2019
Deep Space, Black Hare Press, 2019
Divinity, Iron Faerie Publishing, 2019
Faerie, Iron Faerie Publishing, 2020
Fated, Stormy Island Publishing, 2019
Fear and Fables, Stormy Island Publishing, 2019
Forest of Fear, Blood Song Books, 2019
Guilty Pleasures and Other Dark Delights, Things from the Well Publications, 2019
Harvest 2, Blood Song Books, 2020

MONSTERS, Black Hare Press 2019
Mother Ghost's Grimm Vol. 1, NBH Publishing, 2019
Mythica, Iron Faerie Publishing, 2020
Salty Tales, Stormy Island Publishing, 2019
WORLDS, Black Hare Press, 2019
YEAR ONE, Black Hare Press 2019

Connect
Facebook: @authorjoshuadtaylor
Amazon: amazon.com/author/joshuadtaylor

ABOUT THE PUBLISHER

BLACK HARE PRESS is a small, independent publisher based in Melbourne, Australia.

Founded in 2018, our aim has always been to champion emerging authors from all around the globe and offer opportunities for them to participate in speculative fiction and horror short story anthologies.

Connect

Website: *https://www.blackharepress.com/*

Twitter: *@BlackHarePress*